THE ULTIMATE WAGER

Other CV-2 Books by Raymund Eich

Stone Chalmers

The Progress of Mankind
The Greater Glory of God
To All High Emprise Consecrated

The Confederated Worlds

Take the Shilling
Operation Iago
A Bodyguard of Lies

Novels

The Blank Slate
New California

Short Novels

The ALECS Quartet

Collections

The First Voyages: The Complete Science Fiction Stories
1998-2012

THE ULTIMATE WAGER

Raymund Eich

CV-2 Books • Houston

The Ultimate Wager

Under low, roiling clouds, the electric bus from New Madison crept down the streets of the alien city.

Near the front of the bus, holding onto a ceiling strap, Connor Little peered through the crowd. The Hspa Nki, seven feet tall with bluish-gray skin, walked on two backward legs. Thin glide membranes, translucent and veined, joined the two triple-jointed arms on each side. A light breeze rustled the dense patterns of beads, indicators of rank and role, tied to their tail quills. Their voices struck the bus like a downpour on a metal roof. From the din, Connor's comm implant could only extract the words *vacuum breathers*.

Never mind the planet's natives. Where were the explorers from Earth?

There had to be other humans nearby. A week ago, a ship had descended past the high plateau the human colonists called New Madison, toward this alien city in their planet's lowlands. An Exploration Consortium ship, it had to be. The descending ship must have seen the buildings, farms, and fabs of New Madison.

The crowd thickened. The bus lurched forward a few yards at a time.

No explorers from Earth showed amidst the Hspa Nki.

On an open field beyond a thinner part of the crowd, Hspa Nki threw flying discs made of some thin, pliable material regurgitated by one of the native bugs. The Hspa Nki were left-handed. Their back-hand throws wobbled, but their forehand throws zipped and they plucked passes from the air.

Connor wavered on his feet. These Hspa Nki had failed to be picked for the aliens' ultimate flying disc team.

Explorers from Earth can't help you. You have to win this game on your own.

He rubbed his neck and shook out his free arm. The Hspa Nki had first seen a flying disc a week before, when they'd come up to the plateau to suddenly demand a retroactive land tax. Just because they had taken to throwing and catching the disc didn't mean they grasped ultimate's tactics—offensive stacks, defensive formations and marking, and more. The people of New Madison had played ultimate for thirty years, ever since *Bascom Hall*'s crash on this planet turned them from explorers to colonists.

A Hspa Nki drifted past the bus on spread glide membranes. Lucas, one of the New Madison all-stars, frowned. "Coach, if they can glide like that..."

Connor raised his voice to carry to all the players on the bus. "I insisted to Nednennik, the Hspa Nki's representative, that their players be forbidden from gliding to get open or catch a disc. Or catching with more than two hands. Nednennik agreed."

Lucas eased back in his seat, and the other players relaxed. Good, stay loose, ready to play.

Connor wished he could. Lose, and the New Madison colonists would be expelled from this planet; sent back to an Earth he and the other older colonists wouldn't recognize, and the younger ones, including all the players, had never known.

The bus' air conditioning labored as they approached a gap in a long, tall, knobby structure. Even after they went through the gap and parked in a cavernous garage, the air in the bus cloaked Connor like a steamy bathroom. Then they stepped out and the effect intensified. The air seemed almost chewy.

He inhaled. Chewy, but oxygen rich.

Outside the bus, a Hspa Nki lifted and spread its quills. Its haws blinked over its eyes.

Connor turned his palms up. "Honored host, I am Connor Little, son of…." He rattled off the names of his parents, still alive up on the New Madison plateau, and his grandparents, last seen before he left Earth as a teenager.

The Hspa Nki replied with a long list of ancestors, indicating low rank. "Honored guests, your fellows wait in the preparation chamber." It stretched all four arms toward a rounded doorway.

Connor's whole body quivered, like filings exposed to a magnet. Did the Hspa Nki mean—? "Fellows?"

"Yes." It held its arms in place. "They wait."

On unsteady feet, Connor led the team toward the rounded doorway. Lights inside pulled him closer, but part of him resisted. People from Earth, but why hadn't they come up the plateau to New Madison?

He went into the preparation chamber.

Flexible lighting panels, obviously human-made, clung to the regurgitated-brick ceiling. The panels illuminated two men.

"We've found our lost colleagues from the crash of *Bascom Hall!*" one said. He had thick black eyebrows curling down at the ends. Tall, with ropy limbs, he strode forward. Something about him seemed familiar. "I'm Vijay Rambard."

The room around Connor shrank away from his vision. Autumn evenings, the 3D in his parents' house on Earth. "I watched you when I was a kid. That championship series, against Denver, '72…" Connor's face warmed. A championship series Rambard's team lost.

A wince flickered over Rambard's face. "Always glad to meet a fan. But though I'm proud of my ultimate career, I've been a xenodiplomat with the Exploration Consortium for twenty years." He gestured at the other man. "This is Ernst Gonçalves. One of the Consortium's benefactors." A sour tone crept into his voice.

Benefactor? Some rich man salving his greedy conscience with donations to the Exploration Consortium. Connor's face tightened.

Gonçalves' head, neck, and shoulders flowed together, and his stomach lapped his belt. "You must tell me all about your colony," Gonçalves said around labored breaths. "Surviving a massive hyperjump malfunction, the loss of your ansible and emergency beacon, and a crash landing on an alien planet. Earth's audiences will clamor for your story."

"And you'll take fifteen percent?" Connor asked.

Gonçalves' face soured. "Mr. Little—"

"They aren't here to sell 3D rights." Rambard's tone sliced through the air. "Not everything is about making money."

Gonçalves peered at Rambard through droopy eyes. "I don't need you to tell me that."

Rambard rolled his eyes. "You amassed five billion dollars—"

To Connor, Gonçalves said, "We'll discuss your story later. We have much else to discuss now."

Connor's comm implant flashed a fifteen-minute warning across his vision. "And not much time." He turned to the players. "Change clothes and get ready. Now!"

The players took their duffel bags to cubbies along the far wall. They changed into uniform shorts, jerseys, and cleats, and tossed bottles of sports drinks to one another.

"While the players ready themselves," Rambard said to Connor, "we'll tell you what we know or infer. As soon as our ship entered orbit, the Hspa Nki realized we had much more advanced technology than you were able to preserve from *Bascom Hall*'s wreckage."

Connor bristled. "We've done fine. A fusion reactor for power, a self-driving electric bus...." Obsolete toys compared to what Earth must have developed in the last thirty years. "Go on."

Gonçalves spoke, his words punctuated by heavy breaths. "The Hspa Nki only confirmed to us your colony existed after they imposed on you a tax you could not pay. But apparently they love to wager?"

"We're sure they never saw a flying disc, let alone an ultimate game, before they came up the plateau to New Madison and demanded all our technologies and almost all our production for the next decade."

"Their wager is a negotiating ploy," Gonçalves said. "They offered to waive your land tax if the Consortium paid them ten billion dollars."

Connor's mouth fell open. Finally he found words. "You didn't pay?"

Gonçalves' jowls shook with his head. "The Consortium cannot agree to so large an expenditure in a few days. We all wish it could."

Rambard chuffed out a breath. "Speak for yourself. We don't need to pay the Hspa Nki. Connor, your team will win this game. Because I'll be their coach."

Thick warm air flowed into Connor's lungs. Rambard might be a former star player, but—"I'm their coach."

"I played eight seasons in the North American Ultimate Flying Disc League. Decades later, I'm still in the top ten for many career stat categories."

Gonçalves cleared his throat. "In regular season games."

From under thick eyebrows, Rambard glowered sidelong at Gonçalves. "And I know firsthand how elevation impacts disc flight."

Connor's forehead furrowed. "Flight is flight, right?" Nearby, one of his players nodded.

"You don't leave your plateau, do you?"

Arms spread, Connor quickly said, "The Hspa Nki monitor any-one crossing the perim—"

"You mentioned '72. My last year with Houston. Yes, we lost the finals against Denver. Because there's a mile of elevation difference between Houston and Denver. Discs fly differently in the two cities."

He turned to the players. The young men paused in tying cleats and pulling on jerseys. "Right now, you're two miles below the eleva-tion of the New Madison plateau. Down here, discs will fly differently than you expect. I can coach you through that. Connor, I'm sure he's a good mayor, has great amateur knowledge about ultimate, but if he coaches you today, you'll lose."

Mouths slack, Braden and most of the other players stared through wide eyes at Rambard. Lucas did too. Then he glanced at Connor and quickly turned his head.

As Mayor, Connor had long coached the team, but he could see immediately his players had already chosen their new coach. "I'd be a fool to turn down your offer," Connor said.

"You're no fool." Rambard pumped Connor's hand and slapped his back. "We're going to win this. You heard me, men?" he called to the players. "We're going to win! Hit the field!"

The players cheered and filed out of the chamber. Their cleats clattered on the regurgitated-brick floor. The sound loosened a knot of unease in Connor's gut. He had good players, and luck in having a former pro coaching them. New Madison would win this game.

Only Gonçalves remained in the room. He cleared his throat with a liquid rasp. "Mr. Little, I can't add any value to your team's play. I'll send a report now to Earth via the ansible on our ship. I'll join you on the sideline in a few minutes."

"Take your time," Connor said. "We don't need you."

Gonçalves wheezed in a breath. "A time may come to reconsider that." He waddled away.

Alone, Connor left the preparation chamber. His footsteps echoed off the chewed-and-hardened walls. Hspa Nki with thinly-beaded tails guided him to the field with sweeping gestures of their four arms.

He emerged from the tunnel into the largest enclosed space he'd ever seen on the planet. Scalloped grandstands surrounded the field, rising like the walls of an eroded canyon. Hspa Nki crowded the grandstands. Thousands of clinking alien voices echoed. *Vacuum breathers.* Connor hunched his shoulders, as if the voices were rain falling from the low gray clouds.

At the stadium's far end, a tall wall held panels with gargantuan, unreadable alien script and a twisted structure of curved, nested arms. Three Hspa Nki clung to railings under the text and structure. Connor's comm implant labeled various objects. Team names. Points. Time remaining.

Connor went to the New Madison sideline. Most of the players stretched or made short, soft warm-up throws, all with wary eyes on the steep grandstands.

"We've never played a road game before, have we?" Connor said. He squatted near the players, ran his fingers through the coiled, green-black ground cover, then beckoned for someone to throw him a disc. Though fabricated by the Hspa Nki, and as yellow as the barely-remembered sun of Earth, the weight and feel filled his hand and slotted into decades of muscle memory. "But wherever we play, it's the same field, the same disc, and the same spirit of the game."

Smiles and nods showed among the players. Braden closed his

eyes and bobbed his head at some music played through his comm implant.

Rambard, Connor, and Lucas went to midfield for the opening toss. Two Hspa Nki players accompanied Nednennik, whose tail quills bore a thousand multicolored beads. Nednennik's haws peeled back and it stared at Rambard while its quills rustled.

"Good to meet you somewhere other than the negotiation chamber," Rambard said with a smirk.

Connor stepped forward. "Honored host, are all the rules clear to you and your players?"

Nednennik's voice sounded like a bag of pebbles rolled from hand to hand. "Yes," Connor's comm implant translated to his auditory nerves. "A player scores a point by catching the disc in the opponent's end zone. The possessor of the disc may not run and may only pivot on one foot and throw. The defender guarding the disc's possessor calls out ten seconds. If the possessor holds the disc for ten seconds, or throws an incomplete or intercepted pass or one landing or caught out-of-bounds, possession goes to the defending team. Contact is forbidden. Players call their own fouls, in the spirit of the game."

The humans nodded. The Hspa Nki won the toss.

Back at the human sideline, Rambard told the team, "We're throwing off. Remember! Down here, the disc won't carry as far as you're used to. Who's throwing off?"

Players nodded at Lucas. Sure hands and strong arm, a handler.

"Throw harder on the throw-off," Rambard said to him. "Trust me. It won't go for a touchback. And everyone, on deep passes, the same applies. Throw harder than you think you should. Starters, get out there!"

Braden raised his hand. "Which side do we force them to throw on?"

Since an opponent with the disc could only pivot, and most throws came sidearm, the player guarding the disc-handler would generally stand in one throwing lane to force the disc-handler to throw down the other. Announcing the forced side let defenders marking receivers know from which angle to expect a pass.

A brief frown, dispelled by a shake of Rambard's head. "They're left-handed, aren't they? Force to their left." Their forehand side.

Players nodded. The starting seven ran a couple of steps toward their own goal line.

"No!" Connor shouted.

The players stopped running and jostled together.

"Have you seen them, Rambard? They throw strong forehands. Their backhands are weak. Force to their right!"

Rambard stared at Connor, then turned to the starting seven. "As I said. Force to their left."

Connor's chest burned. Then a firm voice burst through his comm implant. "Honored guests, are you ready to begin?"

"We are," Rambard said. He slapped Braden on the shoulder. "Get out there, men!"

The players ran out to their own goal line. Lucas stood in the center and raised the disc to show his readiness. The golden disc contrasted starkly with the blur of Hspa Nki in the far grandstand. The disc commanded the eye, like a ship at a launch station with the whole galaxy to be explored.

At the far end zone, amid a line of gray-blue figures, the tallest Hspa Nki raised its hand.

Lucas lined up for a backhand throw-off. "Game on!" He swung back his arm.

Connor's throat tightened. Too big a backswing. Rambard must have it wrong. Lucas would throw the disc through the end zone for a touchback.

Face tight, Lucas grunted and whipped his arm forward. The disc came out fast from his hand—

—and flew wrong. Too slow for the power behind it. And though discs curved a little in flight, this one banked like an airplane turning hard to the right.

Connor's stomach fell.

Rambard was correct.

The disc arced toward the right sideline and dropped through the thick air. Hspa Nki loped toward it. Most passed it. The disc landed only a few yards beyond the center line, great field position for the aliens. The humans rushed up to play man-to-alien defense.

A Hspa Nki picked up the disc with its top left hand. Braden guarded the alien, standing in front of the alien to its right and waving his arms. Blocking its backhand passing lane, just what Rambard had called for. "One!" Braden counted. "Two!"

The Hspa Nki pivoted left and snapped a forehand pass. An effortless motion of its elbows and wrist. The disc curled over the sideline, then zipped toward a corner of the end zone. A Hspa Nki strode to the corner and raised its left hands. Lucas matched the alien stride for stride, but the disc curled inbounds past his stretching fingers.

The Hspa Nki squeezed the flying disc between its left hands. Connor's face scrunched up. Good catch, great throw.

The crowd rustled its tail quills and cheered like concrete rattling in a mixer. The human team's shoulders and heads drooped. They trudged to their goal line to receive the next point.

"Rambard!" Connor shouted. "Force to their right!"

Rambard stood stiff-backed. He lifted his palm toward Connor, yet kept his back to him, and his gaze on two players substituting in. He spoke quietly and the two players hurried onto the field.

The Hspa Nki throw-off landed three yards in front of the human goal line. Lucas made a short forehand pass to Tanner. The disc slid through the air to the left—Tanner stretched to catch it. Connor let out a breath. *The team is getting the hang of this—*

Tanner threw a backhand to Dustin. The disc curled away from Dustin and clacked into the ground. Turnover.

One Hspa Nki sprinted for the center of the end zone while a second went to the disc. A high forehand pass and the sprinting Hspa Nki caught it easily. The crowd cheered.

Cold oozed down Connor's throat.

The next human possession ended the same way, turnover and quick score. Hspa Nki 3, New Madison 0. The crowd sounded even louder this time, as if they'd thrown Connor into the mixer with the concrete.

Labored breathing suddenly cut through the noise. Gonçalves took up position next to Connor. "My regrets for my lateness. What is our situation?" He looked at the scoreboard. Hspa Nki scoreboard operators glided from perch to perch. "I see."

The world spun. Connor shut his eyes. "We're getting humiliated."

Gonçalves rested his fleshy hand on Connor's shoulder. "The game has barely begun. The winds of fortune may yet turn."

In a lull of the crowd noise, Rambard's words to the next substitutes carried to Connor. "Short passes on offense until you get a feel for the air density. On defense, force to their right! Make them beat us with their backhands!"

The Hspa Nki throw-off landed four yards in front of the end zone. Lucas picked up the disc while his teammates formed a stack, a line running toward midfield. Everyone looked more assured. One by one, human players broke from the stack to give Lucas passing opportunities. He flicked a forehand eight yards to Dustin, Dustin to Jacob past the fingertips of a lunging Hspa Nki. Back to Lucas. With more short passes, they advanced.

Braden made a sharp cut in the end zone and ran alone toward the sideline. Lucas tossed a soft forehand into the air ahead of Braden. Connor groaned. A throw that soft would drop to the ground before Braden could catch it… if they played up in New Madison. The disc seemed to levitate as Braden ran to it and cradled it in both hands.

Now, the only cheers came from the human sideline.

On the next Hspa Nki possession, the human defense forced them to their backhands. Tail quills rippled, signaling unease. The Hspa Nki backhands traveled slowly and curled off-target. One bounced off a Hspa Nki's right hands. Turnover and quick score for New Madison.

Momentum shifted for the rest of the first half. At halftime the scoreboard showed Hspa Nki 8, New Madison 6.

Connor stared at the scoreboard, looking past the players returning to the sideline. Within striking distance, but could they close the gap?

The players drank water and toweled off sweat. Rambard clapped and aimed an intense gaze at them. "Men, you're getting the hang of disc flight down here. And because you're conditioned for thinner air, you'll have stamina for the entire second half. Keep playing your game, and you'll win!"

New Madison received the throw-off to start the second half. The players sprinted to their positions. Crisp passes sliced through the thick air. Players made sharp cuts toward the disc-handler or into the corners of the end zone. On defense, they hustled to guard the disc-handler and deflected throws off their fingertips. The Hspa Nki managed several points, but with four minutes left in the game, New Madison tied the score at 13. One quick turnover later and Lucas fired a deep pass to Braden in the end zone. Connor's heart soared with the disc.

Braden caught the disc and tapped both feet a few inches inside the sideline.

New Madison 14, Hspa Nki 13. Three minutes to go.

On the next throw-off, the Hspa Nki raced to the disc. Their handler launched a long but wobbly backhand toward a streaking teammate. The Hspa Nki receiver dove. Its glide membranes rippled, then air stretched them out. Its dive seemed to last forever. With its top left hand, it plucked the disc from the air an inch above the ground.

Connor's arm snapped up and his index finger jutted at the play. "Hey!"

Lucas ran up to the Hspa Nki, then swept his head from side to side. His comm implant relayed his words to the sideline. "No gliding. You agreed."

"I didn't glide," the Hspa Nki said.

"Yes, you did." Lucas pulled his arms up, as if to stretch out glide membranes.

"I didn't glide."

Lucas' face turned red. Human players ran up.

"Don't lie!"

"We all saw you glide!"

Hspa Nki huddled around their player. "She did not glide," one said.

Another alien waggled its tail quills and spoke into the ears of nearby teammates. The Hspa Nki soon argued among themselves. Rapid clattering voices and waves of rippling quills erupted, but soon died down.

Connor found himself standing next to Rambard, two yards onto the field. The Hspa Nki wouldn't blatantly cheat—

The Hspa Nki receiver set the disc on the ground, then dragged its tail quills. "Honored guest, my teammate saw my actions better than I could feel them. The disc is yours."

Lucas nodded, then looked at the still-running clock. "We're willing to add thirty seconds for this stoppage."

"What?" Rambard muttered. "Don't offer that." Thirty seconds more for the Hspa Nki to tie the score.

"That is most generous," the Hspa Nki said. "We agree."

"No!" Rambard shouted.

Connor scowled at him. "The Hspa Nki needed time to realize Lucas was right. It's in the spirit of the game to give them time back."

"We wouldn't have done that in the NAUFDL playoffs. Let alone when a human colony on this planet is at risk." Rambard clawed the air, then flung his hands forward. "Lucas offered, they agreed, we can't back out now. Damn." He retreated to the sideline.

Connor followed. His voice flowed like a wide river. "It's the spirit of the game."

"You think because I got paid to play I don't appreciate the spirit of the game?" Rambard shook his head and peered past Connor at the scoreboard. The clock stopped, ratcheted back around its spiral, then restarted.

Gaze darting between the field and Rambard, shoulders hunched, Lucas picked up the disc. "Game on!" he shouted.

Lucas' throw left his hand. The disc quickly turned over and knifed along the ground. He gaped after it.

Don't let Rambard get in your head. Just play—

The Hspa Nki formerly guarding Lucas broke toward the end zone. Mouth gaping, Lucas ran after it, but a second too slow.

Catch in the end zone. Tie game.

The next throw-off went to Lucas. A Hspa Nki with wide arms and quick feet guarded him just outside the end zone. Lucas faked a backhand, then made a soft forehand throw.

The Hspa Nki lunged for the disc. It slapped the side of the disc, keeping it spinning and deflecting it to the end zone.

Eyes wide, Lucas ran after it, shoulder to shoulder with the Hspa Nki. It stretched its top left arm toward the disc while boxing out Lucas with its right elbows. Its fingers clamped around the edge of the disc.

Connor's stomach flopped. Gonçalves' labored breath roared in his ears.

The Hspa Nki led by one.

On the next throw-off, the disc landed between Lucas and Dustin. Lucas shook his head and backed away.

Come on, Dustin, you're a good handler. Connor's thought sounded like a lie told to a child.

Three Hspa Nki raced forward, one to guard Dustin and two to stand five yards back in his passing lanes. Not a double- or triple-team, therefore legal. Dustin's head jerked around, looking for open teammates.

The guarding Hspa Nki's translated shout came through Connor's comm implant. "Eight. Nine. Te—"

Dustin tried a hammer throw to Lucas over the guarding Hspa Nki. The disc dropped like a shot bird.

Two Hspa Nki broke for opposite end zone corners. The third tossed a backhand over Lucas' outstretched hands to its teammate.

Hspa Nki 16, New Madison 14, ninety seconds to go.

Lucas hung his head. He shuffled to a stop and looked to the sideline.

"We should pull him," Rambard said.

"No," Connor said. He caught Lucas' gaze and gestured for him to calm down. "Play your game!" he shouted. To Rambard, he said, "He's the best handler we have. You've seen that?"

Rambard frowned. "That's true."

Connor filled his voice with assurance he did not feel. "Play your game!" he shouted again.

Lucas nodded at Connor, then jogged with growing intensity toward the goal line.

"Men!" yelled Rambard, "you have time to tie the game if you score quickly!"

The Hspa Nki throw-off landed three yards in front of the goal line. Lucas picked up the disc and surveyed the field. Despite the Hspa Nki guarding him, he fired a curling backhand to Jacob near midfield, then hustled up for a drop pass. He zipped a long forehand to Braden in the end zone.

Down by one. A minute to play.

Rambard sent in substitutes with fresh legs. A tie at the end of regulation would send the game to sudden death overtime. New Madison's best chance was a deep throw-off, a quickly forced turnover, and a disc to the end zone.

Lucas raised the disc in readiness. A Hspa Nki matched the gesture. Lucas threw off.

The disc headed toward the right corner in front of the Hspa Nki end zone. Connor gritted his teeth. If the disc landed over the goal line, touchback for the Hspa Nki. If it landed out of bounds, the Hspa Nki would start in the field's middle.

Braden, Quillen, and Waters raced after the disc. It landed inbounds four yards in front of the goal line. Perfect place to crowd the Hspa Nki handler.

Quillen guarded the handler, jumping from side to side and waving his arms. Braden remained five yards upfield, a foot from the sideline, blocking the forehand throwing lane. The Hspa Nki handler pivoted to forehand, to backhand—

"Seven!" Quillen counted. "Eight!"

—to forehand, and threw. Braden leaped. The disc hit his open palm and tumbled to the ground.

"Turnover!" Connor shouted.

Quillen and Waters had already broken for the end zone. The Hspa Nki player dropped back to cover Quillen heading toward the middle, leaving Waters unguarded toward the back corner. Braden picked up the disc.

Connor's breath hitched. Had Braden thrown at all today? *Come on, easy, a firm throw, float it in the thick air—*

The disc spun gently out of Braden's hand. The right throwing lane, but too soft. Like Lucas on the game's opening throw-off, he used muscle memory tuned for the thin air of New Madison. The disc glided downward, far too short for Waters to catch it in stride.

Waters' blue eyes widened. He angled back toward the disc. His cleats dug into the ground cover. The disc sank through the air. Waters stretched. Dove—

The disc clacked against the ground. It rolled on its edge over his arm and bounced into his face, then settled upside-down on the ground.

The crowd's cheers erupted. The Hspa Nki players all looked at the clock and lifted their tail quills in dominance. The human players looked too, hands on knees, eyes haggard.

Three seconds, two, one.

Zero.

The human players trudged to the sideline. Braden turned his shoulders away from his teammates. Tears flowed down his face.

"I lost the game," he said, voice choked.

Connor's arms enveloped him. "We played as a team and lost as a team."

"That's right," said Lucas, his eyes moist. Other players nodded in agreement.

Braden buried his face in Connor's shoulders. "We're going back to Earth because of me."

A labored breath heralded Gonçalves. "The winds of fortune may yet change."

Braden backed out of Connor's hug. His brows crinkled at Gonçalves. Connor glared at the lying billionaire. "Change? How?"

Gonçalves raised a palm. "I must first talk with Nednennik."

Nednennik loped across the field, glide membranes rippling. "A well-played game, honored guests," it said. "You nearly proved yourselves our equals. You must vacate our planet within thirty local days."

Older New Madisonites hadn't asked to be marooned here, but to lose the only home the young generation ever had… Connor shut his eyes. "We wi—"

"A word," Gonçalves said. "Nednennik, you told Rambard and I you would waive New Madison's land tax if we paid you ten billion dollars?"

Nednennik's tail quills flattened. "I did."

Gonçalves heaved out a breath. "I will pay it."

Connor's head swam. His comm implant caught Nednennik's skeptical reply. "You said the Exploration Consortium could not pay that amount."

"It can't. *I* can."

Rambard scowled. "What are you doing?" he hissed at Gonçalves. "Your net worth is only five billion."

"No. It *was*," Gonçalves said. "Just before the opening throw-off, I ansibled our situation to Las Vegas, on Earth. The sportsbook computers gave New Madison odds of 1:2. I wagered almost all my holdings that the Hspa Nki would win."

Nednennik writhed its quills. "New Madison would either win the game or you would pay its debt. Wisely chosen. You, of New Madison and of Earth, are truly our equals."

Amid the knot of players, Braden watched with red-rimmed eyes. His mouth parted in a newborn smile. A wave of understanding flowed from face to face.

The Hspa Nki spectators filed out of the grandstands. The scoreboard operators took down the score panels and spun back the clock's nested arms. Nednennik and the last Hspa Nki players entered the tunnel to the aliens' locker room.

Rambard stared at the coiled, green-black ground cover and shook his head.

Connor went to him. "You coached well."

"Not well enough." Rambard turned his head. "We started off forcing the wrong way—"

"You understood what the thicker air would do to the disc. I had no idea." Connor rested his arm on Rambard's shoulder. "You coached us better than I would have."

Rambard nodded yet pulled away.

Nearby, the New Madison players huddled together, again with tears. Now, though, their tears rolled down faces lifted to the sky and trickled past giddy smiles and laughing mouths.

Connor blinked at Gonçalves. For a man who barely knew them to pay so much... "You spent your entire fortune?"

"Not *entire*. I'll live comfortably enough—"

"But why? For us?" He widened his arms to indicate the players behind him.

"The Exploration Consortium will want to lease base facilities from New Madison, which benefits us both. I will win acclaim on Earth, something a fortune alone cannot buy. And a colony of human beings will keep its home of thirty years."

Pressure welled behind Connor's eyes. "Thank you."

Gonçalves shook his jowly head. "You don't need to thank me. I acted in the spirit of the game."

—The author thanks David Abmayr, Jr., Ph.D. for technical consultation regarding altitude effects on flying disc dynamics and ultimate gameplay.

About the Author

Raymund Eich files patent applications, earned a Ph.D., won a national quiz bowl championship, writes science fiction and fantasy, and affirms Robert Heinlein's dictum that specialization is for insects. Hundreds of papers cite his graduate research on the reactions of nitric oxide with heme proteins. He hasn't played ultimate for many years, but still throws a good forehand.

Connect with the author at **www.raymundeich.com** or scan the QR code below.

Sign up for his mailing list to receive exclusive, pre-release content about his upcoming books. Your email address will never be shared and you can unsubscribe at any time. Go to **www.raymundeich.com/mailing-list** or scan the QR code below.

Other Books by the Author

Available wherever books are sold.

Learn more about these titles at our website, **www.cv2books.com**, or scan the QR code below.

STONE CHALMERS

Earth barely survived the 21st Century. Biotechnological and nuclear terrorism, civil war, famine, and ethnic cleansing killed billions. Thousands fled on warpdrive ships to colonize planets around distant suns.

In the 22nd century, after the United Nations established control over Earth, it opened wormhole links to the distant colonies, to prevent a repeat of the previous century's chaos on a galactic scale.

Enter operative Stone Chalmers. Spy. Assassin. Instrument maintaining the UN's order on the settled galaxy.

Opposing him are hostile forces on colony worlds... and within the UN itself.

When Stone clashes with those forces, the UN—and every human world—will be transformed forever.

Learn more about the Stone Chalmers series at **www.cv2books.com/stone-chalmers**, or scan the QR code below.

THE PROGRESS OF MANKIND (#1)

To maintain order in the 22nd century, the UN relocates undesirables through artificial wormholes onto colony planets. Everyone benefits… except the planets' original colonists.

Now, the newly rediscovered colony of New Moravia learns the UN's plan and fights back.

THE GREATER GLORY OF GOD (#2)

Thousands fled the chaos of the 21st century on rogue warpdrive ships to settle colony planets. When Earth reunified in the 22nd, its fleets rediscovered the colonies and hunted down the warpdrive ships.

Every warpdrive ship but one.

TO ALL HIGH EMPRISE CONSECRATED (#3)

After unifying Earth, the UN has rediscovered the colony of Minerva. Prosperous and technologically advanced, Minerva quickly submits to UN supremacy.

Surprisingly quickly…

IN PUBLIC CONVOCATION ASSEMBLED (#4)

After unifying Earth, the UN controls all human colonies scattered through the galaxy by means of wormholes, warpdrive ships, and ruthless operatives. Operatives working to strengthen the UN.

Or destroy it.

THE CONFEDERATED WORLDS

The purpose of all other combat arms is to put the infantryman in sole possession of the battlefield.

A thousand years from now, while Earth sleeps in virtual reality, three polities—the Confederated Worlds, the Unity, and the Progressive Republic—strive to connect the scattered, terraformed worlds of humankind by artificial wormholes. When they meet, they clash, in a decades-long struggle of arms that will embroil every human world, in which dedication to duty liberates worlds—and oneself.

Learn more about the Confederated Worlds series at **www.cv2books.com/the-confederated-worlds**, or scan the QR code below.

TAKE THE SHILLING (Book 1)

The Confederated Worlds implanted in his brain the skills to make him a soldier. Tomas had to learn for himself how to survive interstellar war.

OPERATION IAGO (Book 2)

The Confederated Worlds lost the war. Can Lt. Tomas Neumann win the peace against elusive, deceptive foes out to turn the Confederated Worlds against itself?

A BODYGUARD OF LIES (Book 3)

Assigned to the halls of power, only Capt. Tomas Neumann can save the Confederated Worlds from the ultimate treachery.

NOVELS

THE BLANK SLATE

Neuroscience entrepreneur Clay Shieffer must stop a tyrannical president... because he unwittingly gave the tyrant power over the human mind.

NEW CALIFORNIA

After New California's founder committed suicide, two men vied to rule the colony.

Ashwin George, supported by the colony's elite and the Chinese company dominating half the settled galaxy.

Against him, Desmond Park, nanotechnology engineer, armed with the most formidable weapon of all.

A single idea.

SHORT NOVELS

THE ALECS QUARTET

He had a month to learn the planet's mysteries—and Juliette's.

His cover story: return to Elard to dismantle his sect's missionary work to the planet's natives.

His true mission: investigate decades-old mysteries of love and death.

His objective: return to Earth with his discovery.

If he can.

COLLECTIONS

THE FIRST VOYAGES: THE COMPLETE SCIENCE FICTION STORIES 1998-2012

From 21st century asteroid settlements to World War II Romania, from an Earth dominated by immortal aliens to Christ's empty tomb, a fresh, distinctive voice in science fiction will take you on journeys to the photosphere of the sun, the coding regions of DNA, and the complexities of the human psyche.

www.ingramcontent.com/pod-product-compliance
Lightning Source LLC
Chambersburg PA
CBHW051928220626
47052CB00003B/631